April 8, 2012

lax,

Happy Easter!
Look forward to hearing you
read to me soon.

xox   Love, xox
        Nini + JJ.

Copyright© Irene Klitzner, 2010

All rights reserved. Except as permitted under
the U.S. Copyright Act of 1976,
no part of this publication may be reproduced,
distributed, or transmitted in any form or by any means,
electronic, mechanical, or otherwise, or stored
in a retrieval system, without the prior written permission
of the publisher and author/illustrator.

Attitude Pie Publishing
1835 NE Miami Gardens Drive #121
North Miami Beach, Florida 33179
www.AttitudePie.com

ISBN: 978-0-692-01275-8

Library of Congress Control Number: 2010918512

Printed in the U.S.A. by
BookMasters, Inc.
30 Amberwood Parkway
Ashland, Ohio 44805
January 2011, M8105

Happy Whistling!
xoxo
Irene K.

THANK YOU
to all who whistled while I worked!

Steve, my love, who listened, and listened,
and listened, and listened...

Adam and Joshua, for their patience and love,
even when I cooked their meals with my pen!

Mom and Dad, who always encouraged me to
be creative and write.
They are smiling from above...

Bern and Har, for always loving everything I do.

Sean
Age 6

And, to the real Sean Michael K., my son,
who 21 years ago, at the age of 6,
was a laugh a minute,
trying to learn how to whistle.

Sean Michael K.
Today

Sean, did you really think you could whistle IN the moon?

Sean Michael K. Whistles the Wrong Way!

by Irene Klitzner

Illustrated by
Carrie Lou Who

Attitude Pie Publishing
Miami, Florida

This is the story of Sean Michael K.,
who was trying to whistle
one hot summer day.

2100

Sean had a problem
that quickly arose.

He mixed up the way
that the whistle goes.

Instead of **out**, he whistled **in**.

That's when his troubles began to begin...

While chewing a chunk
of pink bubblegum,

Sean did something silly,
but so, so, so dumb!

He blew **in**
a whistle,
the gum
whizzed

d
o
w
n.

In went his grin
and out came a frown.

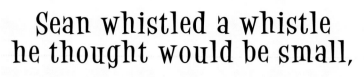

Sean whistled a whistle
he thought would be small,

but somehow, he somehow
gulped down a big ball!

ervous he grew,
nd his whistle did, too,
hen suddenly
smelly, old shoe
ot through!

CHIRP
CHIRP
CHIRP

He tried,
oh he tried,
but he could
not avoid,

down into his
tummy went his
parakeet, Floyd!

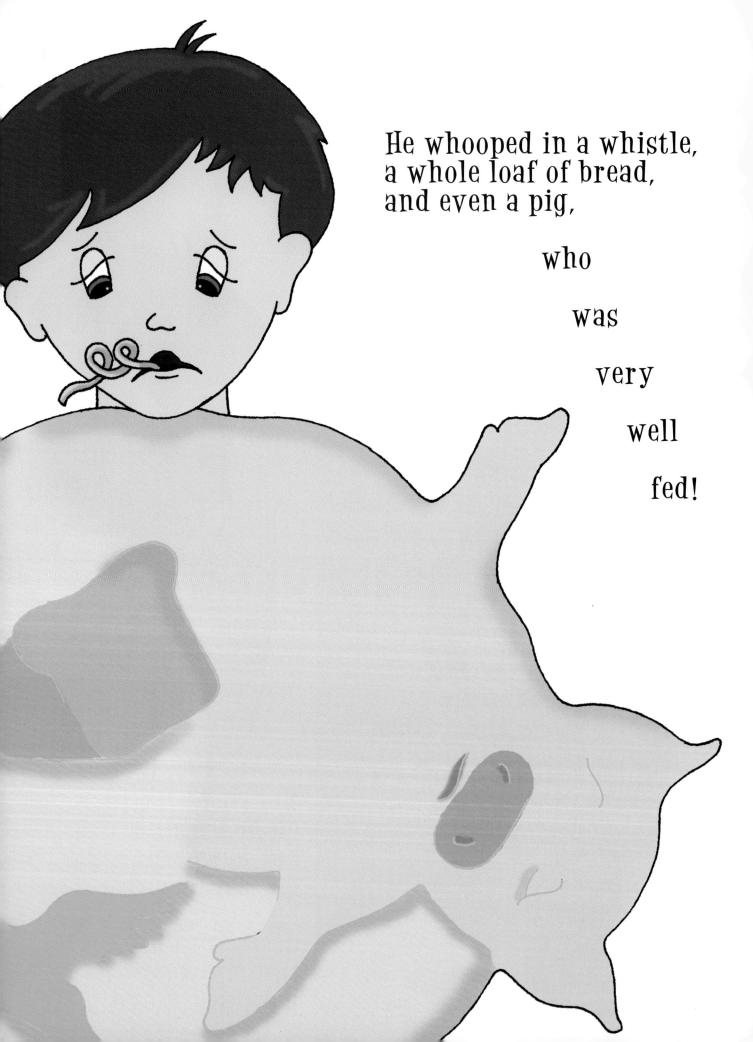

He whooped in a whistle,
a whole loaf of bread,
and even a pig,

who

was

very

well

fed!

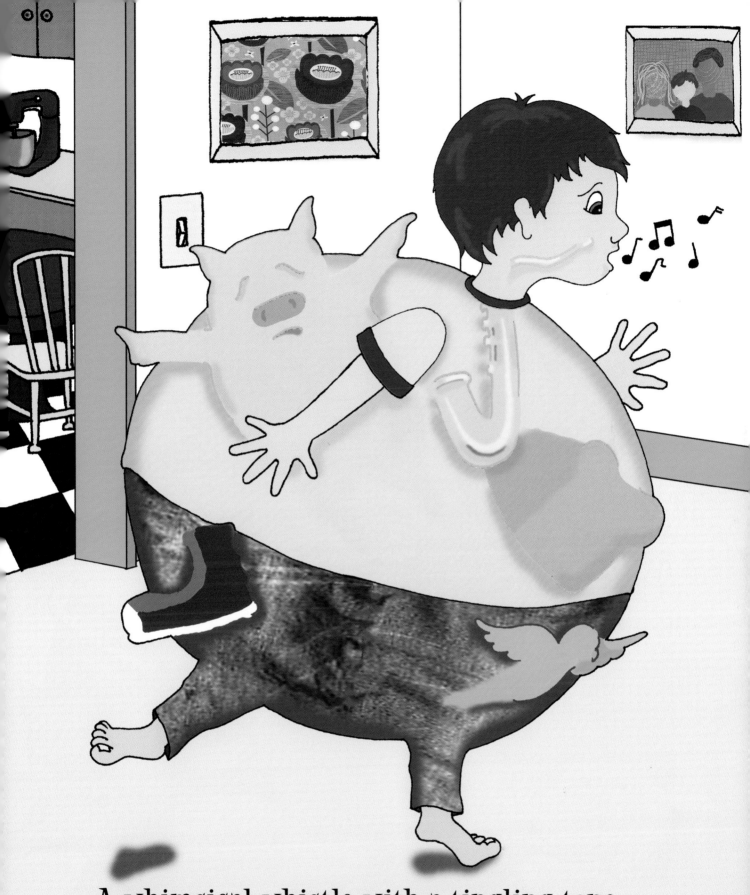

A whimsical whistle with a tingling tone,
and down slipped Sean's new saxophone!

Can you believe how big Sean grew,
when IN, IN, IN, he blew, blew, blew?

This wackiness boomed in the laundry room.
With a whopper of a whistle, he sucked in a broom!

Suddenly, Sean

Sean

REALLY

began to expand...

When
the moon
beamed in,
he no longer
could stand!

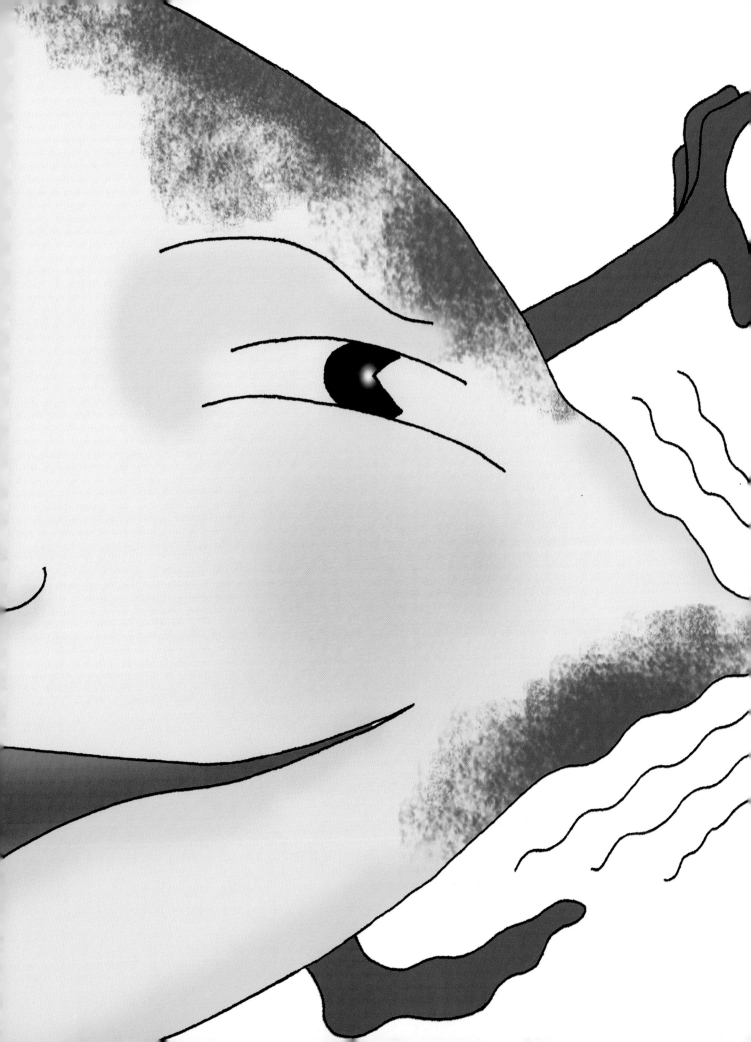

THE MOON?

The moon!!!

It went down with a

Zoooom!!!

"OH NO!!"
he moaned,
as he filled
up the room.

"Enough is enough!
This must
come to a stop!

If I whistle
in more,
I am likely to
POP!"

All of a sudden,
Sean Michael K. knew,

there was just one thing
for him to do.

His best friend, Spencer,
was a whistling champ.

He won 17 trophies
at Whistling Camp.

Sean bounced out the door
and across the grounds.
It felt like he weighed about

one MILLion

pounds!

Over,

under,
around,
and
through,

THIRD AVENUE

'Til he rolled to a stop
at Third Avenue.

There at the house
of Spencer G.,
Sean popped up
and hollered,

"HURRY,
HELP ME!!"

I've tried all my tries;
cannot do it right.

My whistles take IN
whatever's in sight!"

"Spencer, be a pal,
and show me just how,

to quit with the

in

and whistle

out now!"

"Sean, you know I'm a pro,
I'll unmix your blow.

There are
66 whistling tricks
that I know."

Sean tried to do
what Spencer G. said,
but no whistle came out,
only hot air instead.

"No! No!" Spencer screeched,
"You can't grit your teeth.
Keep your lips out in front
and your tongue underneath."

Sean whistled like a missile
and sooner than soon...

Kaboooom!!!
Zoooom!!!

Out
Shot

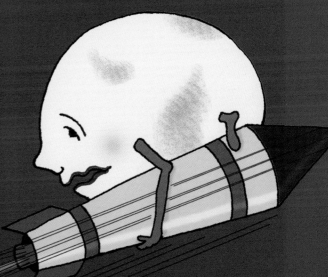

the moon!!!

His confidence boosted,
taking over his gloom,

then, quick as a hiccup,
he brought out
the broom!

He whistled his
saxophone out
with pizzazz;

a sassy sound of jazz
it sure has!

The bread spun out in the shape of a bun.
"This whistling business is really quite fun!"

Now that he knew what to do as he blew,
out flew Floyd, who was whistling, too!

Things were all happening so very

fast.

That stinky,
old shoe
blew out
with a

blast

Sean certainly knew
what was next to come,
because all that was left
in his tummy was

He whistled and whistled, but nothing came through.
"It's stuck like glue, Spencer, what should I do?"

"Sean, trick 22 is my best advice:

Just whistle **in** once,

then whistle **out** twice."

Again, Sean did
what Spencer said,
but the gum did not pop,
it stopped instead.

Tightly his lips were
so gripped with gum,

"Mm-Mm-Mm-Mm-Mm-
Mm!"
was all he could hum.

Just then,
a rare noise
blared into the air.

Spencer's eyes grew wide
with a startled stare.

Sean was blowing a

gi - gan - tic

bubble,

that **BURST** with a

BANG

and brought him more trouble.

Gobs of pink gum
were glopped on Sean's face.

In fact,

gobs

of

pink

gum

were

all

over

the

place!

Do you think this could stop him?
Well, just take a guess...

Sean puffed out his chest and whistled right through the mess!!!

So, now you have met
Sean Michael K.,
who learned how to whistle
one hot summer day.

Sean no longer has trouble
when he whistles about.
Of course,

hopefully

he's learned,
not IN, only OUT.

But, if you should meet him
one day or one night,

just in case he forgets...

by Irene Klitzner

Illustrated by Carrie Lou Who

hold this book
REALLY tight!

about the author

Irene Renner Klitzner was born and raised in Miami, Florida. After graduating from the University of Miami with a degree in Elementary Education, she happily took an amazing adventure through motherhood with husband, Steve, raising 3 wonderful sons, Adam, Sean, and Joshua. Currently, she and talented business partner, Peggy Adams, design and manufacture a line of children's clothing called Attitude Pie, in stores worldwide. Along the way, Irene met illustrator, Carrie Lou Who, and their imaginations joined hands to create this whimsical book, but the real Sean Michael K. and his pal Spencer G., couldn't have been any funnier trying to whistle, one hot summer day, back in 1989.
That's how it all began to begin...

about the illustrator

Carrie Lou Who grew up as number six in a family of 15 in Racine, Wisconsin and her passion for creating things has led her to the wonderful path she now travels. She received her BFA from Milwaukee Institute of Art and Design. Currently, she is living her dream of working from home in Milwaukee, WI. Carrie's amazing life today is shared with her husband, Rich, and daughter, Lola.